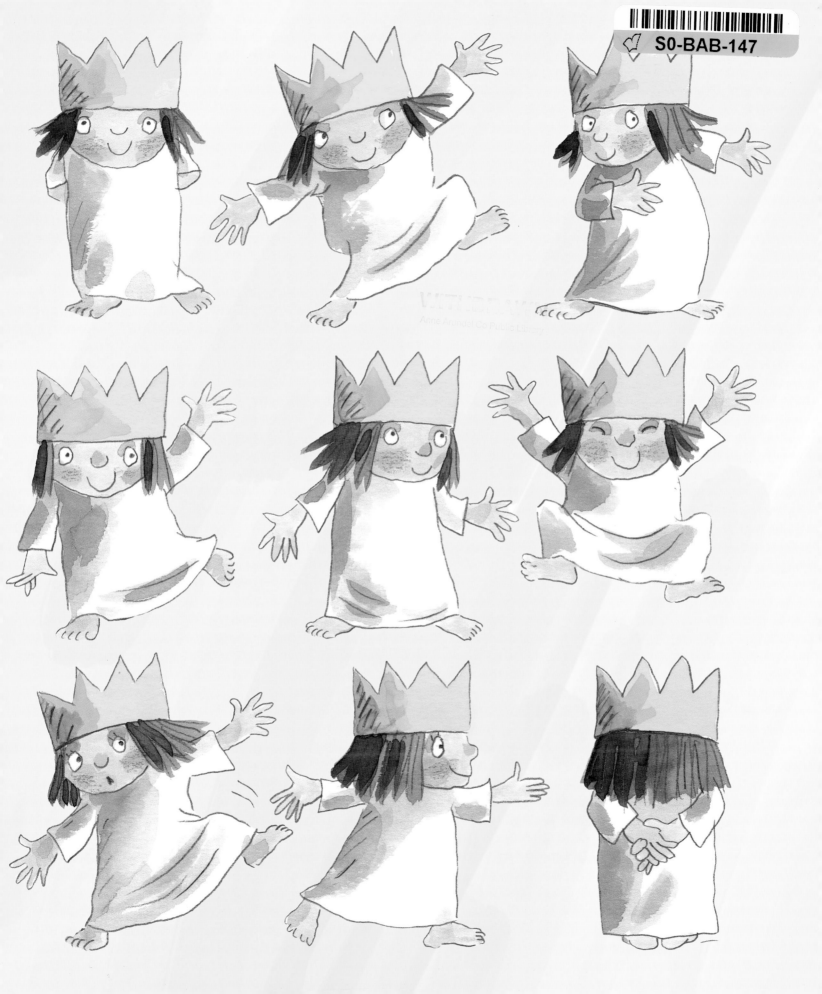

To Arie and Nell

American edition published in 2018 by Andersen Press USA,
an imprint of Andersen Press Ltd.
www.andersenpressusa.com

First published in Great Britain in 2018 by
Andersen Press Ltd., 20 Vauxhall Bridge Road, London SW1V 2SA.

Distributed in the United States and Canada by
Lerner Publishing Group, Inc.
241 First Avenue North
Minneapolis, MN 55401 USA
For reading levels and more information, look up this title at www.lernerbooks.com.

Color separated in Switzerland by Photolitho AG, Zürich.
Printed and bound in Malaysia.

Library of Congress Cataloging-in-Publication Data Available.
ISBN: 978-1-5415-1453-9
eBook ISBN: 978-1-5415-1460-7
1-TWP-8/1/17

Little Princess
I Want My Dad!

Tony Ross

Andersen Press USA

The Little Princess was proud of her dad, the King.
He was taller than all the other dads.

Except when the other dads stood up.
Then, the Little Princess became a bit jealous.

The Cook was taller than the Little Princess's dad,
especially with his hat on, and he baked his son
the most wonderful cakes.

Even the dog would not eat the famous
burned-black cakes that her dad baked.

The General taught his son to ride a pony.

But whenever her dad went near animals (even her mouse) they made him sneeze.

The Admiral taught his daughter to swim.

But the King needed water wings in the bath—
he never swam, he just sank like a stone.

The Gardner took his twins on
adventure walks in the forest.

The King got lost on his way to bed.

"I wish my dad was as much fun as other dads!"
the Little Princess wailed to the Maid.

"I wish he could teach me to ride and cook and swim and take me on adventure walks. He's useless."

"I can teach you all of those things!" said the Maid.

So, the Maid taught her to trot on her pony.
But the Little Princess fell off and bumped her head.

Then the Maid showed her how to make a cake.
But the Little Princess's cake was so hard, it hurt her teeth.

Then the Maid taught her how to swim.
But the Little Princess swallowed lots of horrible water.

Then the Maid took her for an adventure walk in the woods.
But the Little Princess got them lost, so they missed their tea.

The Little Princess felt cold, she felt wet, her teeth hurt, her head-bump hurt, and she was very, very hungry.

She also felt that she couldn't do anything properly.
In fact, she felt quite miserable.

Just then, the King walked by with the dog.

"I WANT MY DAD!" the Little Princess squealed,
rushing up to him. "Dad, I'm useless."

"What can you mean?" said the King, hugging his daughter.
"When I heard about you doing all of those exciting things . . ."

"I felt so PROUD!"

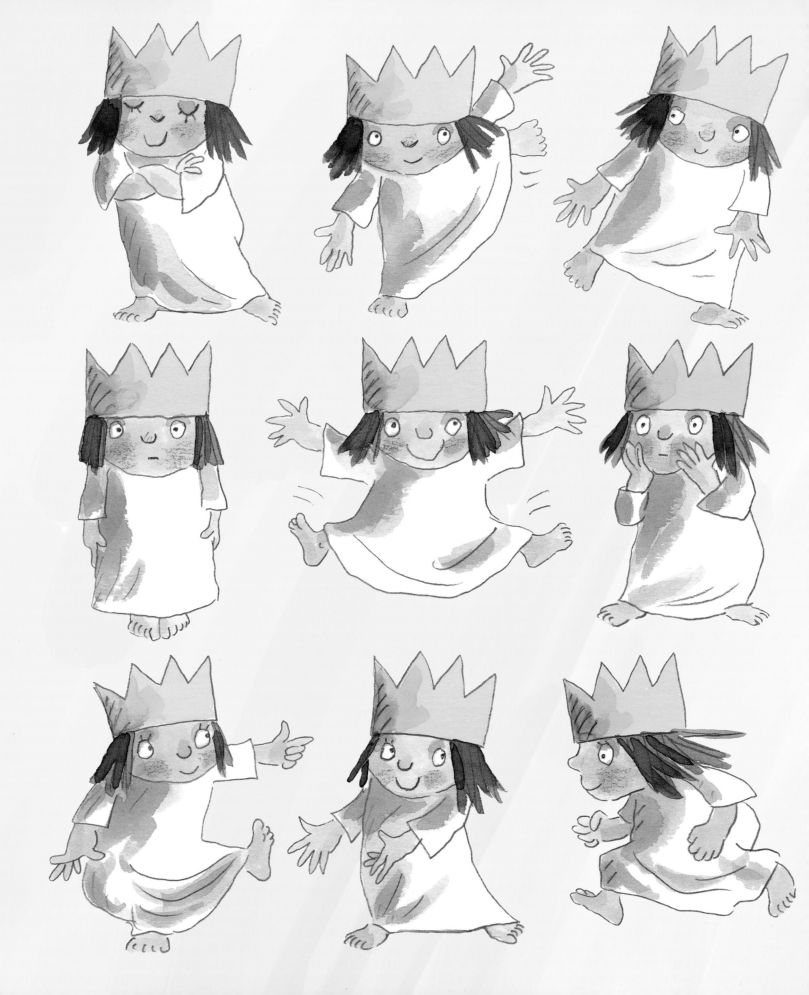